Buddy: From His Home to Yours

BRENDA GRABB

PAGE PUBLISHING, INC.
New York, NY

First originally published by Page Publishing, Inc. 2019

ISBN 978-1-64584-879-0 (Paperback)
ISBN 978-1-64584-880-6 (Digital)

Printed in the United States of America

With all the blizzards slowing down their progress, Buddy and Button are making headway toward arriving for the Christmas Season! While they used to travel by sleigh, of late, they have realized the comfort of cabin travel and especially like to upgrade!

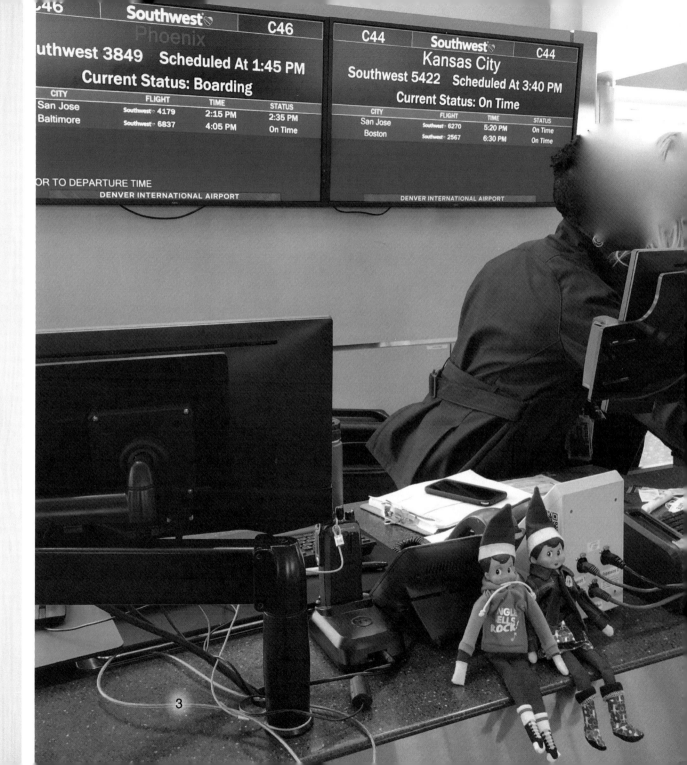

The elves cast their vote for their Voice favorites!

Buddy remembers the birds when it is cold, keeping their feeders filled. Wait—Buddy—what happened? I hope a large bird doesn't come and carry you off!

5

Button is helping Buddy who is feeling a little under the weather. It looks like he has not been making the greatest nutritional choices lately!

Buddy and Button catch up on some of their favorite TV shows, at times making sure they do not have too much Christmas joy! :-/ #thisisus

Raccoon Party!

8

The elves put out some snacks for their old friends, Smokey and Bandit, and their family!

9

Buddy and Button help set up the wildlife nativity set (there is a fox and a raccoon).

Button watches the birds and other wildlife in the backyard (no, she is not spying on the neighbors!).

The elves create hygge for Christmastime!

Buddy and Button have a romantic getaway! (It might have been more romantic with silk pj's rather than flannel, though)

13

Buddy and Button make sure that

14

not one of their friends goes hungry!

Nutcracker Elf defeats the Mouse King! Who knew Buddy could do ballet?

Buddy and Button help decorate the tree with a few of their favorite ornaments.

The elves enjoy some winter fun!

*The elves
practice
their bird
photography,
working together
to get some
great shots!*

Buddy and Button help make sure all the Christmas cards are sent out on time.

Buddy decides to add some highlights to his hair for the holidays!
Button wishes that she could, too, but her hat is not yet removable.

Button thought they were just window shopping at Tiffany, but Buddy

decided to give her a very special Christmas gift a little early!

The elves spy some amazing
goodies at Caffetteria!

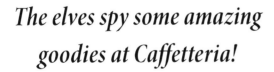

Sometimes it feels like you almost need to be
a superhero to get everything done for the
holidays. It's nice to get help from one! Button
helps bring in all the boxes from the doorstep.

It's a Bundt!

Buddy and Button bake
a cake for Mrs. Claus.
Mrs. Claus: Thank
you! What is it?
Elves: It's a Bundt.
Mrs. Claus: A bun?
Elves: Bundt!
Mrs. Claus: Bunk. Bunk.
Elves: Bundt!
Mrs. Claus: Bun-n-n-t.
Elves: Bundt! Bundt!
(Santa whispers to Mrs. Claus)
Mrs. Claus: It's a cake! Thank
you! Thank you very, very much!
(she turns away, disgusted).
There's a hole in this cake.
—My Big Fat Greek Wedding

25

The Elves Attend the George Winston Concert

Buddy and Button have a night out on the town. George Winston at the Kauffman Center, Kansas City! They were so inspired, they brought their musical memories alive at home!

27

Button would like to wish everyone, TGIF!

Buddy remembers the real Reason for the Season.

Buddy and Button visit the aquarium.

The fish seem quite intrigued.

The elves help build a feral cat house
for their friend, Charcoal.

Elves enjoy Starbucks, too.

32

Elf-sized wine!

Buddy and Button are putting in a few last-minute calls to Santa. Is there anything you just remembered you needed?

The elves hang their stockings by the chimney with care, in preparation for Santa's coming!

Inspired by the amazing Nutcracker ballet, Button tries out some en pointe moves at home.

Buddy and Button find a moment for peace and quiet amid all the last-minute Christmas preparations.

Buddy enjoys a little holiday wine tasting!

No, Buddy! Don't kick that ball!

The elves felt Santa probably had had his fill of milk and cookies
and that a gourmet treat might assure more gifts!

The elves are having a hard time
falling asleep in all the excitement!
Wait, was that Santa?

Merry Christmas morning!

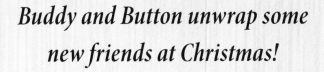
Buddy and Button unwrap some new friends at Christmas!

43

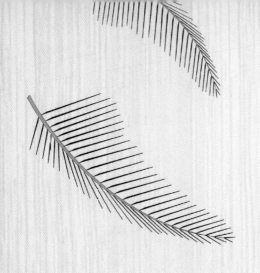

Buddy and Button appreciate each other's gifts!

Buddy and Button head back through the elf portal unit next season. Be good!

Photos and creativity by Brenda Grabb

I would like to thank my family and friends who have been long-time solid supporters of the elf and all his antics and who have encouraged his continued activities and his ultimate appearance in a book! I would also like to thank my publishing coordinator and everyone else at Page Publishing for making this book a reality!

About the Author

Brenda Grabb is a mother, wife, physician, photographer, and lover of all living things—especially wildlife, cats, and birds. She enjoys bringing a smile to others through her photography.